Red Shoes with White S[...]

By
Carol Pavelin & Stephanie Conroy

Picture by Dennis Pavelin

Inspired by our happy childhood in Portishead, England.

Dedicated to the memory of our loving parents Dennis and Beryl Pavelin.

WOODHILL WHISKERS (TM)

Woodhill Whiskers, created by Sisters.

MAP OF WOODHILL

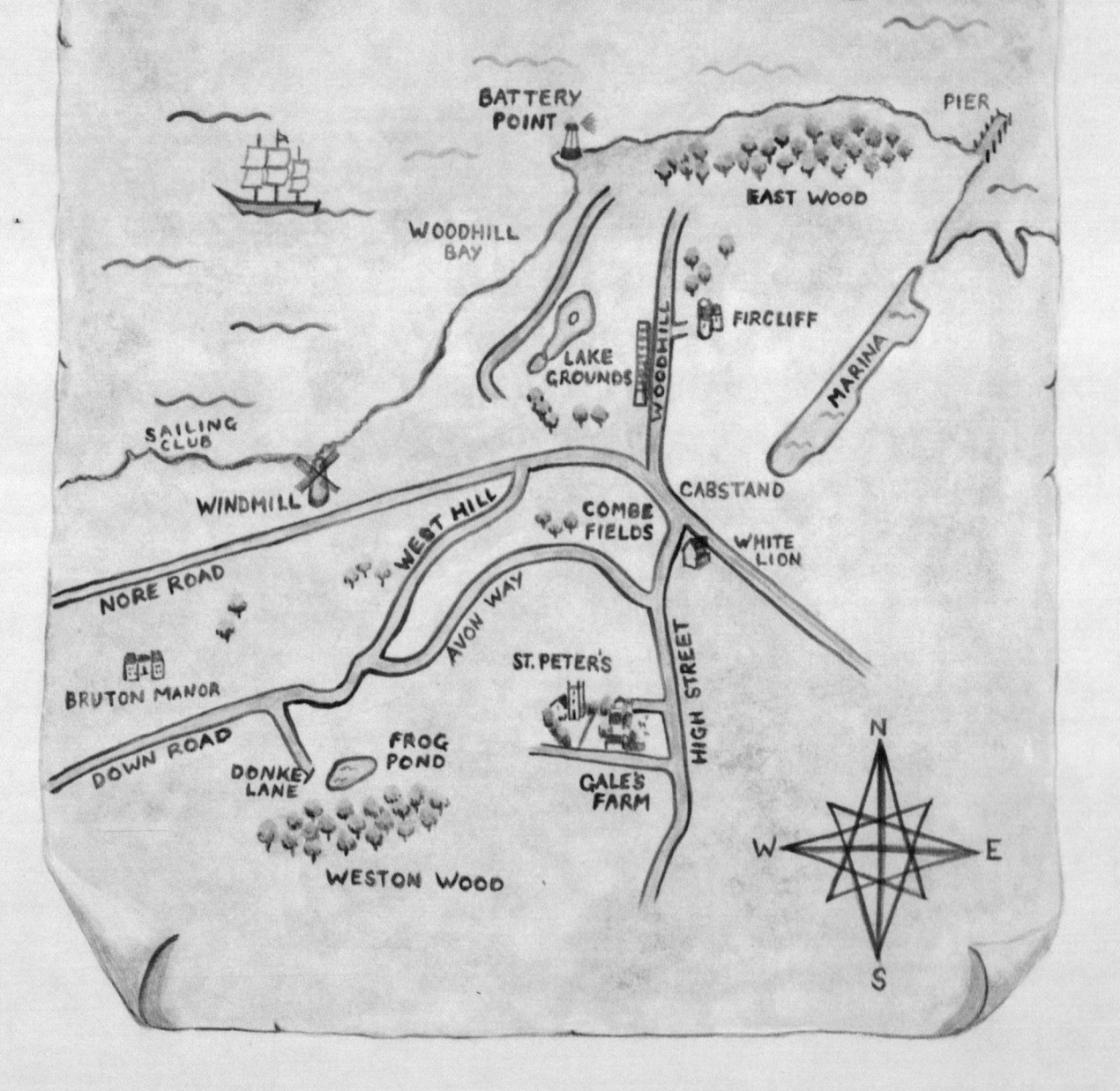

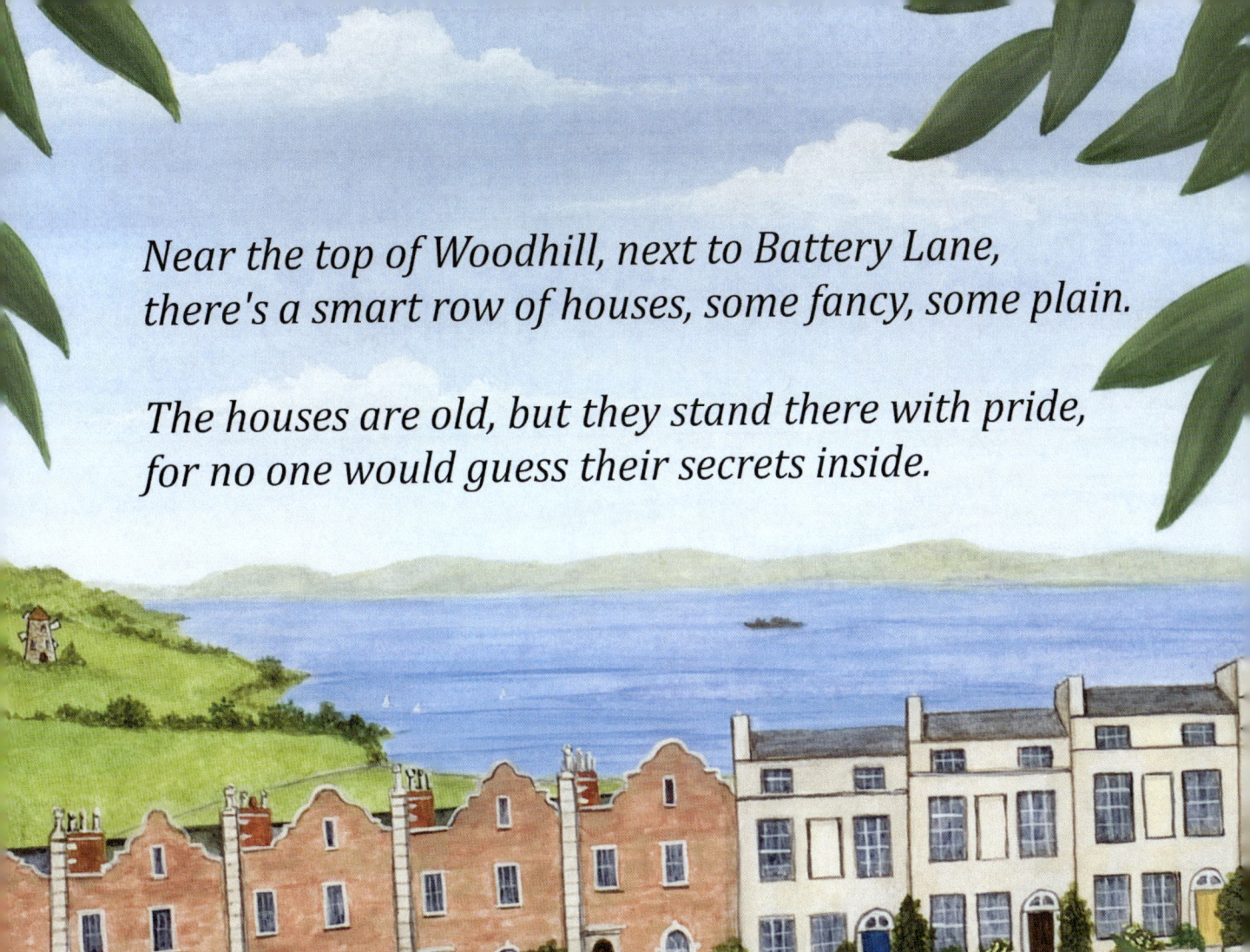

Near the top of Woodhill, next to Battery Lane,
there's a smart row of houses, some fancy, some plain.

The houses are old, but they stand there with pride,
for no one would guess their secrets inside.

There's a scamper in the garage,
a squeak in the shed,
a glimpse of a movement,
when you turn your head.

Deep in the cellar,
at the front of the house,
if you look very closely,
you might see a mouse.

There's a secret mouse house,
with a secret mouse door,
a little mouse mat,
on a little mouse floor.

*There's a little mouse mum, and a little mouse dad,
two little mice girls, and a little mouse lad.*

*So, there's Timothy Twig,
who's talented and tall,
and there's Beautiful Bertha,
like a big fluffy ball.*

*And last but not least, not rounded or long,
there's Giddy Glinda, who gets everything wrong.*

The sun was shining, it was early May.
There was a lot of excitement on that particular day.
For the time had come to buy some new shoes,
and all the young mice
had been told they could choose.
The plan was to be ready
at a quarter to nine.
They wouldn't need scarves
as the weather was fine.

Dad was there first,
with his bright blue cravat.
Mum put on lipstick,
and was wearing her hat.

Next came Timothy Twig, with his little rucksack,
followed by Bertha, with bows down her back.

But where was Glinda?
It was now time to go.
She couldn't be found,
they looked high and low.

*Close your eyes and count to ten,
Giddy Glinda is missing again.*

There she was in a world of her own,

making friends with a beetle
who was all alone.

"My name is Rosemary,"
the beetle did say.
"Can we play together,
for the rest of the day?"

"I am Glinda, how do you do?
I'm off to the shops now,
but you can come too."

*They left on the roller,
just as a treat.
Down Woodhill and Cabstand
to the village High Street.*

They arrived at the shop, that was shaped like a shoe,
with lace at the windows and a door that looked new.

When they looked inside,
there were shelves full of shoes.
There were yellow ones,
red ones, purples and blues.

Timothy chose trainers;
he liked black and white,
but what he liked best
was their bright flashing light.

Bertha chose sandals,
they were a beautiful blue,
with bows on the toes
and a little heel too.

Then Giddy Glinda squealed with delight,
for she'd found some red shoes with squiggles of white.

*They needed to check
that the shoe size was right,
neither too loose,
nor too tight.*

*Glinda was told
to walk down the aisle.
You could tell she was pleased
because of her smile.*

She walked and walked
across the floor.
She walked past the shelves
and right out the door.

She walked and walked
along the street.
All the time she
was watching her feet.

*She walked to Gale's Farm and right through the gate.
All she was thinking was "Aren't these shoes great!"*

She walked past the horse, all covered with flies.

She walked past the cow, with her big brown eyes.

She walked past the sheep, with their white woolly coats.

There were chickens and ducks,
and even some goats.

But Glinda
hadn't noticed
the clucks
and the moos.

She was
too busy
watching
her shiny
red shoes.

She had not
seen the pig,
even though he was fat,
but worst of all she had not seen......

...the CAT!

It's a well known fact, but a sad fact for some,
that when a cat sees a mouse, he just thinks "YUM."

The cat had green eyes
and big paddy paws,
but also large teeth
and nasty sharp claws.

The cat stood there crouching,
with a trace of a smile,
he knew he would pounce
in a very short while.

Glinda was alerted
in the nick of time,
by a sharp eyed robin
with his warning chime.

*She was able to run
to a very small hole,
conveniently close
and made by a mole.*

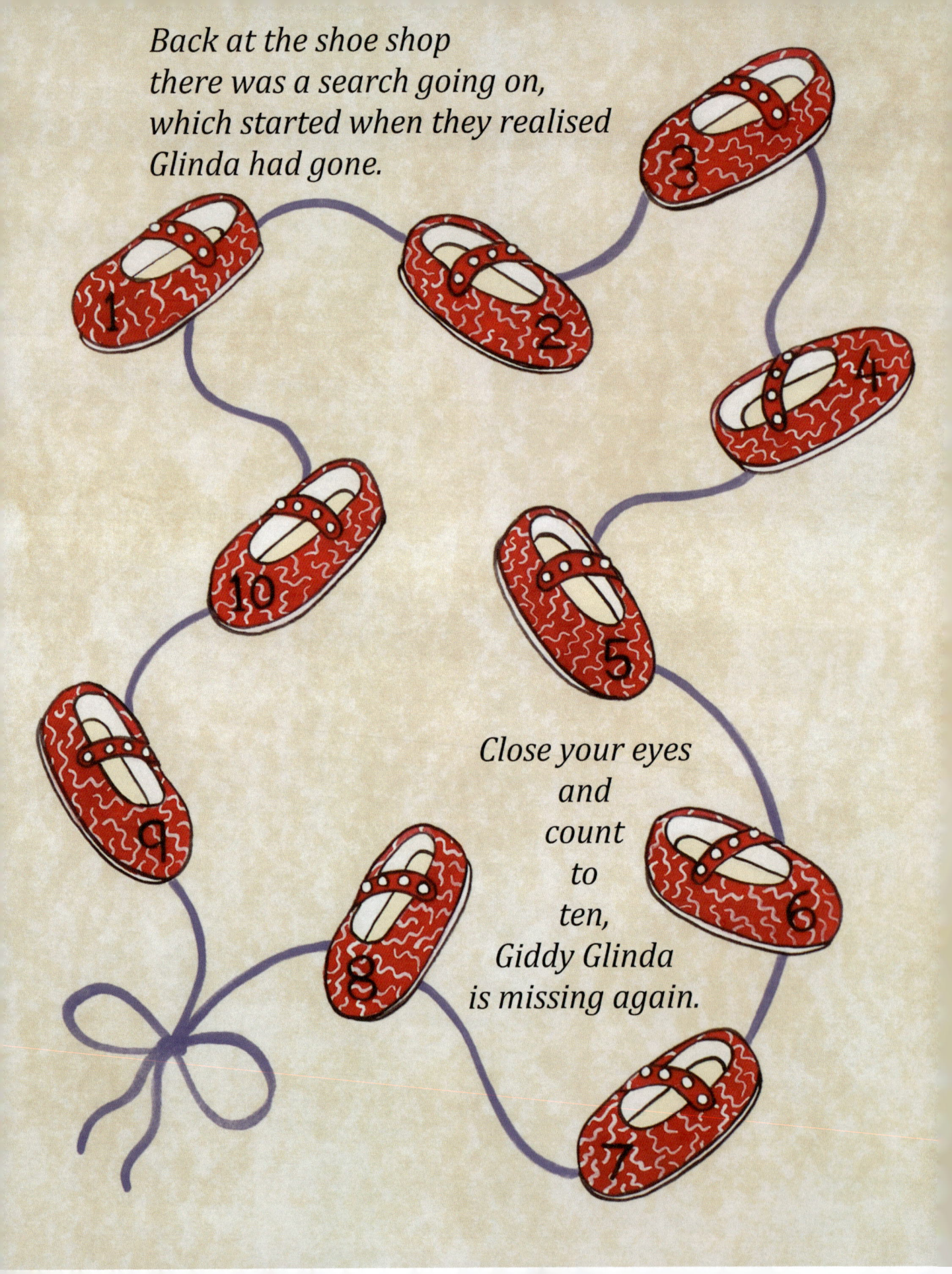

Back at the shoe shop there was a search going on, which started when they realised Glinda had gone.

Close your eyes and count to ten, Giddy Glinda is missing again.

They looked and looked around the floor.
They looked past the shelves.
They looked out the door.

They looked at each other, then they frowned, because Giddy Glinda couldn't be found.

*The cat sat by the hole,
content in the sun.
Playing chase with a mouse
was his type of fun.*

*Glinda stared at the paws
with claws underneath.*

*She stared at the mouth
with the great big teeth.*

*All she could do
was to shiver and wait.*

*She hid there
and wondered,
"What will be my fate?"*

*Then a big black shadow came over the ditch.
It was a rook or a crow, she couldn't tell which.*

*The bird, who was cawing,
attacked the cat from the side.
Who then scampered off,
to find his own place to hide.*

If Glinda was quick, she could escape from the cat.

There was no time to look at the pig that was fat.

There was no time to notice the clucks and the moos. There was even no time to think of her shoes.

She ran past the chickens, ducks and the goats.

She ran past the sheep, with their white woolly coats.

*She ran past the cow,
with her big brown eyes.*

*She ran past the horse,
all covered with flies.*

*She ran out of Gale's Farm and right through the gate.
All she could hear was her rapid heart rate.*

*She ran and ran
along the street.
She was running so fast
she could not see her feet.*

*She ran to her family,
with their arms open wide.
She hugged them all,
and then she cried.*

*She looked at her shoes,
which she had all but forgotten.
They were covered with mud
and smelt a bit rotten.*

*The tears that were flowing, because of her fright,
splashed down on red shoes with squiggles of white.*

*Mum made things better, as Mums often do.
Everything was cleaned, including each shoe.
Dad made them laugh, in that special Dad way,
suggesting fun things to do
for the rest of the day.*

*When the shadows were stretched
by the sun shining still,
five tired little mice
were climbing Woodhill.*

*Bertha was puffed out
and her bows were untied.
Timothy's rucksack bulged
with goodies inside.*

*Glinda was skipping
and humming a song,
watching her shoes,
dancing along.*

*To the secret mouse house,
with its secret mouse door.*

*With its little mouse mat,
on its little mouse floor.*

Then the family of mice, with their sleepy heads,

*had some supper,
and went to their beds.*

*Glinda was dreaming all through the night,
of shiny red shoes with squiggles of white.*

*They reminded her of her best friend, called Bubble,
such fun to be with, but could lead to trouble.*

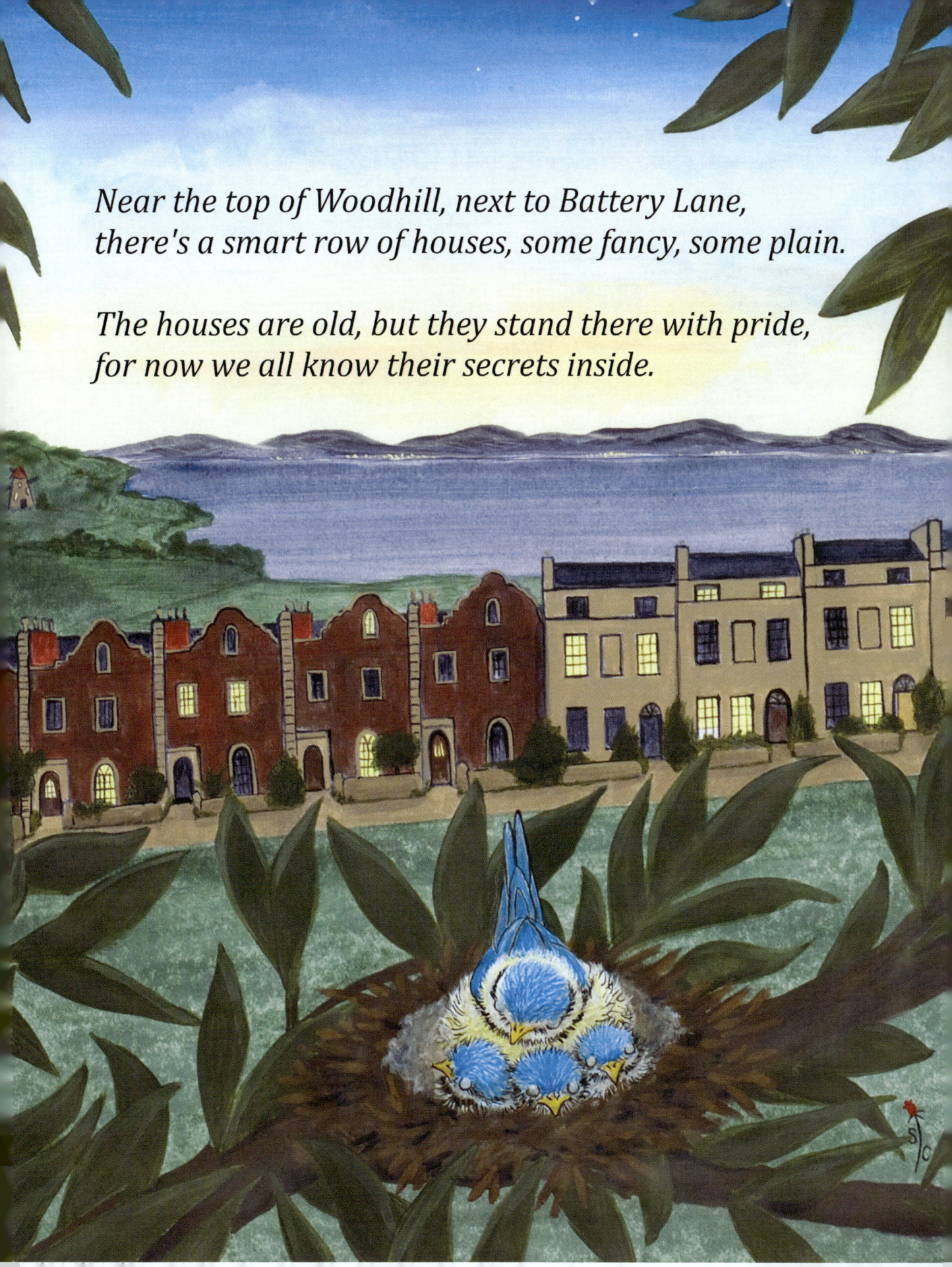

*Near the top of Woodhill, next to Battery Lane,
there's a smart row of houses, some fancy, some plain.*

*The houses are old, but they stand there with pride,
for now we all know their secrets inside.*

The End

Free colouring pages available at:
www.WoodhillWhiskers.com

Made in the USA
Charleston, SC
18 October 2013